Rooster Summer

Rooster Summer

Robert Heidbreder

Illustrations by Madeline Kloepper

Groundwood Books
House of Anansi Press
Toronto Berkeley

Groundwood Books / House of Anansi Press
groundwoodbooks.com

We acknowledge for their financial support of our publishing program
the Canada Council for the Arts, the Ontario Arts Council and
the Government of Canada.

Canada Council   Conseil des Arts
for the Arts   du Canada

ONTARIO ARTS COUNCIL
CONSEIL DES ARTS DE L'ONTARIO
an Ontario government agency
un organisme du gouvernement de l'Ontario

With the participation of the Government of Canada
Avec la participation du gouvernement du Canada | Canadä

Library and Archives Canada Cataloguing in Publication

Heidbreder, Robert, author
Rooster summer / Robert Heidbreder ; illustrated by Madeline Kloepper.

Poems.
Issued in print and electronic formats.
ISBN 978-1-55498-931-7 (hardcover). — ISBN 978-1-55498-932-4 (HTML). —
ISBN 978-1-77306-137-5 (Kindle)

I. Kloepper, Madeline, illustrator II. Title.

PS8565.E42R66 2018   jC811'.54   C2017-905303-5
                          C2017-905304-3

Jacket and interior illustrations by Madeline Kloepper
The illustrations were created using inks, gouache, graphite
and digital technique.
Design by Michael Solomon
Printed and bound in China

MIX
Paper from
responsible sources
FSC
www.fsc.org   FSC® C012700

To my grandma and grandpa and
all the hard-working farmers
of yesterday and today.
RH

For the long summers in the cul-de-sac.
MK

Table of Contents

A Noisy Good Morning

A cocky morning crowing
and a daybreak braying.
A snappy-tap rapping
and a nose-nudge tapping.

Grandma ups
the window sash,
and in struts Rexster,
up off Seed-Sack's back,
over his head,
straight across the floor,
fluttering onto beds.
"He's gonna peck!
He's gonna peck!"
we both shout as we spring up and out.
But one last rooster-doodle-doo,
and Rexster swooshes through the window,
past Seed-Sack's swaying,
straw-hatted and still-braying head
and back onto his back.

Our summer days of farming fun
    have noisily begun.

Egg Hunt

"Egg hunt! Egg hunt!"
Grandma grins, handing us
straw-softened baskets
for morning eggs.
"Be quick now!
Quick sticks! Quick sticks!"

Rexster greets us in the hen yard
on the slow swaying back
of Seed-Sack.
Then, with a feathered swoop,
he's up off Seed-Sack's head, up over ours
and down to the ground.

Gently, we squiggle up onto Seed-Sack,
baskets upended in hand.
Seed-Sack slow-steps
off toward the chicken coop.
We hug-hold tight
for a few steps and … down he sits.
We slide off in a bundle of chuckles.
He turns, brays a big toothy smile,
shakes his old straw hat —

bits drift off like summer snow —
and then stands back up.
Again, again, again
we ride and slide,
slide and ride,
till we tumble down,
smack-front-dab at the chicken-coop door,
upturned egg baskets now hats on heads
and Rexster roo-da-doodling at our sides.

The Chicken Coop

We stoop
into the chicken coop.
This is quick work,
a stinky-hot, feathered fluster-bluster.
Cranky hens flip-fly off their nests,
filling the air with fuss and feather.
Robbers, we scoop and dash
with the biggest and best.
Covered in a flurry of feathers,
like rowdy-night pillow fighters,
we rush out to the fresh, bright morning
and to Rexster and Seed-Sack waiting.

Back

Back up on Seed-Sack's back,
we soft-shimmy,
patting his hatted head.
Seed-Sack grabs
both eggy baskets in his big teeth,
and off we set, slowly,
back to the farmhouse.
Rexster leads the way,
king of the morning parade.

Without once sitting down,
Seed-Sack delivers us to the kitchen door

and sets the baskets on the porch.
We pat-pat Seed-Sack and carry the baskets
into the kitchen to Grandma.
"My two quick sticks!
You were slow as new calves
at fresh salt licks!
Hmmmm?"
"Seed-Sack. He kept …" we start explaining,
just as Grandpa, home from chores,
comes in, wide grin, and says,
"You can't tell with a mule.
They follow no rule."
We giggle, giggle, say it again, again,
over and over, till breakfast finally quiets us
    down.

The 11:58

A flutter and a flap —
and Rexster's in the barnyard,
high on Seed-Sack's hat.
They fast-foot it to the farm gate,
Rexster egging them on,
Faster … faster!
Grandma grabs the wheelbarrow.
We cram in with loud laughter
and thump-bump after.
Grandpa's already there
with pots, pans,
rough and wild hats
and a wobbly chair.
He has a corncob pipe behind each ear.

Train tracks cut the farm in two,
front and back,
like two shiny silver slivers of a stream.
We hear chug-chugs, choo-choos
getting nearer and nearer.
We stuff our shoes
onto our hands.
Pots, pans, funny hats on heads, we wait there.

Grandma rocks on the wobbly chair,
banging more pots, high in the air.

Rexster sits a-doodling on the topmost fence
    post,
while Seed-Sack turns his hind-end to the
    tracks,
wiggle-waggling, his tail swipping
back and forth, back and forth.
Swift as water, the train whips by.
Shoe-handed, pan-and-hat-headed,
we wave, shout and clang out *Hi!*
Faces stare, fingers point, necks crane.
One man drops his soda pop.
We see his mouth open and eyes bug
in a big OOOOPS!

Then it's over.
The train heads off to the city,
as we double up in laughter-bright delight.

"City folks on the go
need a barnyard show,"
Grandpa says.
In a rag-tag line
we shuffle back,
singing high and low.
"City folks on the go
need a barnyard show!"

Our Watermelon

Grandma's garden grows colors:
strawberry reds, cauliflower whites,
eggplant purples, watermelon greens.
One watermelon is bigger, rounder,
longer than all the others.
We love seeing, feeling this watermelon.
If we're in the garden,
or just rumbling past,
we sing out:
> *Grow, melon, grow —*
> *big, sweeter, sweet!*
> *For a treat ... to eat, eat, eat.*
> > *Yum! Yum!*

Sometimes we dance
around it in a ring, chanting,
but sometimes we just pat it,
softly humming,
"Grow, grow, grow."

"When will it be ripe?"
we often ask. "When?"
And Grandma always riddles us back,
"When summer days grow
low and slow, slow and low.
Then you'll know.
Then you'll know."

So we wait.

Barn Play

We scurry up the ladder to the steep hayloft,
grab the long thick rope
and send ourselves flying —
singly, doubly or triply —
while Rexster claw-grips ahold,
fling-fluttering away.
Sometimes we hurl ourselves
into the spiky pile of hay.
Sometimes we just swing
fast to slow to slower to slowest to stop,
and then we hop-drop
as near to Seed-Sack as we can,
full-body patting him as we land.
He loves to try to pull
our shoes off as we fall.
We loosen them for an easy grab.
When he gets one,
he tosses it wildly or squat-sits on it
for a game of mule hide-and-seek.
We giggle-grin, Seed-Sack barn-brays,
Rexster roo-da-doodle-doos.

Barn Cats

The barn hides cats.
Not too far away,
some invisible cats
softly mew-mew
in work and in play.

"Them cats are workin' cats.
They catch mice, bugs, rats,"
Grandma and Grandpa warn us.
"Don't make 'em your pets."
But we do, or try to.

Most scat-cat away
when they sense us near,
but not the one we call Tuftin,
a spiky-haired, white
and light-brown girl cat.
If we lie very still, silent, calm
and put a few grains in hands,
sometimes, just sometimes,
she will pad near, purr, lick us and cuddle.
We don't try to pick her up —
we just let her find comfort with us.

We stroke her soft warmth
and drift off in catnaps with her
in the dusty dark of the barn.

Being quiet as mice can also be nice.

Barking the Cows Home

"Arf arf ruffy ruff!"
Grandpa's barking for us.
We quick-leap from our catnap
and bounce up to him, panting
and barking back,
"Arf arf ruffy ruff!"

His trusted old farm dog, Karmie,
died a few months back,
and he doesn't have a new dog yet.
"Gotta get the right doggone one,"
he smiles,
"or herding'll be no doggone fun."
So for now, we're the dogs,
two-legged tall,
barking the cows home.

We head off to the open pasture,
Rexster and Seed-Sack at the back.
We stand far and safe behind the cows
and dog them back to the barn.
"Arf arf ruffy ruff!
Arf arf ruffy ruff!"

After Suppertime

Tummies all stuffed,
after-supper chores done,
Grandpa grabs a ragged barn blanket
and spreads it out in the barnyard
so we can stargaze and star spot.
We love seeing the Big and Little Dippers
and trying to count the stars.
"One, two … skip a few … ninety-nine … ten
    zillion …"

Soon we're tuckered out,
on the edge of sleep.
Grandma and Grandpa cradle us in their arms,
carrying us to beds, softly singing,
"To beds, to beds, our sleepyheads."
We pj up as Grandma pounds pillows.
We snuggle down in the crinkly sheets
that smell of farm sun, earth and wind.
Rexster's at the window.
Seed-Sack's off somewhere,
still daring to bray the day away
and having his say at deepening night.

We drift off,
wrapped in the farm's musical sway,
and hear far, far away
the 9:53 streaming back from the city,
whistling, choo-chugging away
another farm day.

Mom and Dad

At summer's start, Mom and Dad
visit us at the farm almost every day.
"Are you okay? Are you okay?"
they ask again and again.
And again and again, we say,
"Yes, yes, we're okay!
Plus, plus, plus!"

So little by little, bit by bit, they leave us
to our newfound farm life
with Grandma and Grandpa.
But every Sunday, at 5:30 on the dot,
they arrive for supper
and become part of our summer story,
of Rexster, Seed-Sack
and play-away days.

We know they want us to know
that we can also grow
apart from them, in our own ways,
like crops freshly planted
in fertile fields.

The Storm

Our town friends visit.
It's a hot, hot day.
Down to the creek
for a bit of cool-water play.
Rexster follows
with flaps, flutters and hops,
roo-da-doodling all the way.
Behind him Seed-Sack softly mule-sways,
laughing out his loud mule brays.

First we wade, then plunge deeper
where the creek runs fuller and wider.
Our clothes get soaked,
so we wiggle them off
and slosh them into a pile.
We giggle at the plop-pop sound
they make as they flop down.
Suddenly sun's done,
the whole sky deepens with dark,
lightning jags down ragged forks.
Rough thunder sky quakes all around.
We know to run,
flee the trees and water.

"Lightning's dangerous.
It's sky fire coming to earth,"
Grandpa and Grandma often warn.
We grab Rexster, hug him tight,
wrapping his wings as we hurtle back.
But the 11:58 is streaming down the track.
Dripping wet, we hip-hop foot to foot,
willing it to pass fast.
Seed-Sack hoot-toots a long song
with the train whistle,
head tossed back like a mule playing dog.
All the train folks stare,
pointing, laughing, covering mouths.
We're not that funny, we think as the train
     fades.

We make a dash for the farmhouse.
Grandma and Grandpa
break into long, loving laughter
when they see us.
"Birthday suiters," they tease.
Quickly we realize we have no clothes on.
They're still heaped deep at the creek.
We laugh, point too,
just like the train folks do.

Wrapped in towels and sheets,
we wait for the storm to pass,
then dressed in fresh clothes,
we race back to the creek
to finish our play-away day.

The Fox

"Egg hunt! Egg hunt!"
Grandma beams, handing us
the straw-softened baskets.

We rush into the hen yard headlong,
but something's wrong.
All is quiet, still.
Rexster is perching high atop
the old mulberry tree, his special spot.
He's quiet too — too quiet,
and Seed-Sack's sitting,
alert to all around but us,
his long ears a-twitch.
Slowly, carefully, we push
the door of the coop open —
feathers floating, flung all about
like an inside feathery snowstorm.
Cracked eggs litter the floor,
some spots and drops of blood too.
We run to get Grandma,
who just says softly, "Fox."
Inside the coop, she shows us
where the fox got in.

We get hammers, nails, wood,
and work to make it strong and good.
"Foxes, they gotta eat too, I guess,"
Grandma whispers,
a little sad, we think.

Life in the barnyard can sometimes be hard.

The Stranger

It's raining tough nails.
We run through the barnyard,
shaking wet hair
like a wild mule's tail.
Rexster flit-flitters in circles, wings askew.
We flutter-flap, twirl round too,
elbows crooked out wide.
Seed-Sack stands mule-still,
long head tossed back,
full big mouth open,
drinking deep the rain.
We, too, gulp down
the big hard drops
before we dash into the barn's dark.
We want to make a safe, dry tent house
with bales, poles and the old barn blanket.
We shimmy to the hayloft
up the wriggling-swinging rope,
yank the old blanket from a heap
and …
     a strange man leaps up.
He looks wild, scared, shaky.
We try to scream,

but our voices leave us, like in a dream.
"Shhh! Shhhh!" he whispers
in a voice that sounds like barn straw to us.
"Please bring me some food. Please!
I won't hurt you. I'm just hungry. Please!
Then I'll go. I promise."
We look at him, one another,
and both think we can't say no.

We dart out of the dusty light,
through the barnyard,
where Seed-Sack and Rexster
are still hard at their rain-day play.
When we get to the house,
Grandma's in the cellar.
So, quickly, without telling her,
we grab some cookies, bread, butter,
leftover cold chicken and milk.
We stash it under our clothes
and dash back to the barn.
The stranger takes the food
and eats like we've never seen anyone eat
     before.
We're uneasy — don't want to see more —
so we race back out the barn door,
worried if we've done wrong or right,
right or wrong?
"How long will he stay?" we wonder.
"How long?"
And "Do we tell? Do we tell?"

Spilling the Beans

Grandma's making us a snack.
"You're quiet," she says.
"Quiet as a pack
on the back of Seed-Sack."
We laugh a little,
and then we start to cry.
Grandma takes her hand towel
and wipes our eyes dry.
"Spill the beans," she whispers.
"Spill them all."
We tell her through thick tears
about the scared, hungry stranger in the barn
and what we did.
Then we ask again and again,
"Was it wrong? Was it wrong?"
Grandma rings the big brass dinner bell
out the kitchen window to get Grandpa.

When he comes, we tell him our story.
He and Grandma take our hands gently
and lead us quietly, lovingly to the barn.
At the door, we pull back,
but they both press us on, up to the loft.

The sad, hungry man is gone.
He's left the milk jug and a short note too.
In crumpled, rough letters it says,
    "Thank you."
Under the paper is a piece of rough wood.
It's whittled to look like a rooster toy.
"Rexster! Rexster!" we clap-chant together.
We shed our fear and bounce in joy.
"No," Grandpa says.
"You didn't do wrong. No wrong.
But next time just tell us
to come out and along.
Okay?"
"Okay?" Grandma adds.
"Okay! Okay!" we say,
enfolded in hugs.

Corn Talk

It's a muggy, still night after the rain,
air thick with lightning bugs.
Rexster flips and dips about wildly,
trying to feast on bug bounty.
"Will his tummy glow?" we ask.
"Will it glow?"
"With a Rexster rooster,
you never know.
You never know,"
says Grandpa with a smile
that's warm and slow,
just like the night.

Seed-Sack lets the bugs gather in his ears,
then with a fast shudder-shake
and a mule-head shrug
scatters them back to the night air,
a tiny bright hailstorm of bugs.

Grandma and Grandpa wheel us
down to the corn fields.
We each go in a different row,
steady, silent and slow.

"Shhh! Shhh!" we signal,
and then we listen, all, all ears.

"Shhhh! Shush! Shhh! Shush!"
the growing cornstalks answer
as fresh new leaves unfurl, uncurl …
slow … slow
in no rush, no rush at all.
We reach out, touch the leaves, the stalks
and their gentle babylike plant hairs.

We feel them grow along our fingers.
We pretend to grow too,
up on tiptoe, up we go,
unfurl slow, our fingers like leaves.
We stay long into the lightning-bug bright,
until we're ready for a sleep-tight night.

We snuggle in beds. Whispering corn fills our
    heads.

Ginger-Tea

Rexster's huff-puff crowing!
Seed-Sack's loud bray-blowing!
And we fast-track it out of bed
to stick heads out our window.
There's a dog below, not a puppy — bigger.
We crash down the stairs in pj's
and rush onto the lawn.

Early, Grandpa drove out and away
to get a new work dog for the farm.
"It'll keep that fox at bay!"
says Grandma.
"Can we name it? Can we name it?"
we shout, springing about.
"It's a she," says Grandpa.
"Sure, you can name her for me."
All at once, we both shout out,
"Ginger-Tea."
Grandma and Grandpa scratch their heads,
wrinkle noses and eyeball us hard.
"That was fast — fast as a train going past!"
they chuckle.

We just shrug, slant-glance at one another
and plead, "Please! Please!"

We don't say that many a lazy day
we talked about naming a new dog.
And we think they probably don't guess,
but they probably do.

Ginger-Tea is a perfect name,
since her coat is tawny, spicy-looking
and full, like a lion's mane.

We play with her
with no thought of breakfast.
We run, jump, hide,
cuddle, twist and turn.
We play away
any way we can think of.
We forget about Rexster and Seed-Sack,
who slowly, separately head off,
away and back.

Making Amends and Friends

Noisily, busily, happily,
we're playing with Ginger-Tea.
Grandma and Grandpa call us over
and gently say they think
we're being unfair.
We feel a sudden chill
in the hot summer air.
"Why? Why?" we plead and stare.
They simply point.
We see Seed-Sack and Rexster
at the barnyard gate, left out,
watching us, just watching.
Right away we understand.
We've left out and behind our first
animal friends, our loving pals.

We scoop up Ginger-Tea
and carry her to Seed-Sack and Rexster.

They back-step off when we come.
Carefully, we put Rexster on
Ginger-Tea's back.

Ginger-Tea stands still and then hound-
    bounds.
Rexster leaps off, then on, then off.
A game of tag-fun has begun.
With careful, slow steps, Seed-Sack nears.
He nudges Ginger-Tea, who springs up
and tries to get his hat.
He'll have none of that
and circles her, then stops flat.
Another spring up, another miss.
Seed-Sack trumpets his mule blast,
jerkily tosses his hat off himself,
then noses Ginger-Tea in a wet mule kiss.

Friends, all.

Kittens

We explode into the barn
with shouts and roundabouts,
but something, we feel,
is new, strange, changed.
We can read barn sounds like books now.
"Is the hungry stranger man
around about again?"

We tiptoe,
up and down we go,
all ears, only ears, we tiptoe.
Listen, just listen. *Shhh!*
Slight, light rustling,

scratchy sounds.
We follow them to find
Tuftin and five kittens.
They mew, tumble, stumble,
high-jinks-somersault
one on top of another,
alive with play.

We love their antics.
We watch, watch,
and then we, too, kitten-play,
copycatting the time away.

The Attic

Some cooler days
we do attic play,
where trunks, boxes, corners
are full of come what may.
We love the old clothes,
toss them on any which way
and play, play, play —
school, storybook people,
tough-talking city folk,
fancy-pants rich guys,
hoity-toity dancers at a ball.
This we like best of all.
We crank up the old phonograph
and waltz around to scratchy tunes.
Sometimes Grandma comes in
with an old tin tray,
saying it's the best silver, and serves us
fizzy drinks in the best glasses,
pretending she's a real classy lady.
We bow, take the drinks
and sip without dripping a drop.
As we dance round, up, back, up, back,
we hear Seed-Sack below,

low-braying like a tuba in a brass band,
and Ginger-Tea's soft clarinet-like strand.

When we sneak Rexster inside
(which Grandma doesn't always like),
he jumps on the record
and rides round and round,
wings fanning in, out, up, down,
his scratchy-scratchy doodle sounds
and rooster dancing
rhythmically matching the voice
and beat of the song.
We warble along,
happy in our pretend,
not wanting it to end.

Treasure

We follow the creek farther down
where it twists in curves around.
Here it is shadier, denser,
the creek a bit fuller, deeper.
Maybe we're even on another farm.
Up on the creek bank, where it's steeper,
are small dugouts, cavelike.
"Maybe there's treasure," we hope.
"Treasure!"
We bravely poke
heads in a deeper, darker cave to look,
but we can't see anything,
so we reach in hands,
grasp, grab, grope
and pull out some … BONES!

We drop them with a shriek,
even though they are small, dried.
"The chicken,
the fox's chicken,"
we shout as we fast-splash up the creek
to tell Grandpa and Grandma our news,
so glad, so glad
that this once, this once,
Rexster didn't follow us.

A So-Long Hay Ride

It's a star-bright night,
good for a goodbye ride.
Grandpa hitches Seed-Sack to an old wagon,
soft and prickly with hay.
In we climb with Grandma and Ginger-Tea.
Rexster rides rooster-regal next to Grandpa,
roo-da-doodling like it's early breaking day.
It's mule-stop-and-go all the way,
but we don't care. We throw the hay
all about, burying ourselves,
stuffing it in our clothes
like living scarecrows.

Seed-Sack trundles us past the barn.
We sing-song, "So long … so long,"
and softly mew-mew at the barn cats.
We chug-chug-choo-choo byes
across the railroad tracks
down to the creek,
where we all somersault out
to the night-cool wet of the water.

Grandma pulls
our song-watermelon
out of the wagon.

We cheer, sing its song,
and then all feast —
Rexster, Seed-Sack, Grandma, Grandpa and
    us —
on the sweet treat,
spitting the dark seeds
into the starry night.

Up into the wagon we scramble.
On past the chicken coop,
a steady mule-step back to the house.

We keep sing-songing,
"So long … so long,"
as the night farm sighs
a summer-gone song.

Good-Morning Goodbyes

A cocky Rexster crowing,
a Seed-Sack braying
and a Ginger-Tea barking.

Grandma ups
the window sash.
In flaps Rexster,
behind leaps Ginger-Tea,
while straw-hatted Seed-Sack nods,
neck long-stretched through the open window.
We both shake ourselves awake,
more slowly, more sadly too.
Today is goodbye day —
to the farm,
to our animal pals,
to Grandma and Grandpa,
to summer.
We pat, hug,
snuggle, cuddle, again, again,
knowing how much we'll miss them all.

A Surprise

Grandpa comes back in with a box
full of small holes.
He's grinning sky-wide.
Without a word, he hands it to us.
It shakes a bit and stirs.
We open it carefully.
Inside is a bundle of purrs.
It's one of Tuftin's kittens from the barn.
It soft-winks at us,
then springs up into our laps.
We laugh away our leftover cry
and hug the kitten tight.
It's warm, toffee-tuft bright.

"What do you want to name him?" Grandpa
    asks,
as we both quickly shout out,
"Summer! Summer the Cat!"
Summer tumbles
over in furry, purry fun,
mewing a soft "friends-for-sure yes."

Mom and Dad come in the takeaway car.
We scramble in to the loud bray-doodle-barks
of Seed-Sack, Rexster and Ginger-Tea.

We wave wild goodbyes
to Grandma and Grandpa,
to our true forever friends all around,
as Summer the Cat,
our new mewing pal,
summer-purrs us back to town.

School Reports

We have to write
about summer for school.
"Nothing bad.
Nothing sad.
All things glad!"
recites Miss Neftell.

We decide to write about
Rexster and Seed-Sack,
one taking one, one the other.
"Stories take away worries!"
Grandma often says.
So we think it's good
to stretch stories a bite and a bit,
as you should,
making the full most of it.
"It may not have happened exactly like that,
but still it's as true as a farmer's big hat,"
Grandpa always adds.
We want our stories
to make Miss Neftell and our friends
happy and glad.

Seed-Sack

Seed-Sack is a mule who thinks he's a horse, or a human, a rooster, or a dog. He gives us slide-rides because he likes to sit down when we try to ride him. Then we plop on the ground.

It's hard to teach a mule tricks because Grandpa says, "You can't tell with a mule. They follow no rule." But we taught Seed-Sack to carry baskets of eggs, to play tag and to toot along with the train that goes by. He also nuzzles the barn cats and hides our shoes when we play in the barn.

He wears an old straw hat, which he once gave to Ginger-Tea, the dog. But she didn't wear it right, so he took it back. Then she wanted it back. So now they share and are friends. We taught them that too.

We can't wait to visit him again on the farm. He's too big to go in the trunk of the car, or the truck, Grandpa says, and besides he might get hurt.

His other best friend is Rexster, the talking rooster.

Here's a Seed-Sack rhyme Grandpa likes to recite:

Seed-Sack, Seed-Sack, old and gray,
open your mouth and loudly bray.
Lift your ears and blow your horn
to wake the world this sleepy morn.

The End

Rexster

Rexster is a farm rooster who can talk. He says, "Get up, kids. The sun is shining. Get up!" Every morning he says this because we taught him how.

He follows us everywhere. He plays with us in the barn, swings on the rope and helps us gather eggs. He sometimes shares his food with the barn cats.

We like Rexster a lot and miss him. But Grandpa and Grandma say we can visit anytime. He can't come visit us though, because he lives on the farm and should stay there.

His best friends are Seed-Sack the mule and Ginger-Tea the dog. He likes to hitch rides on both of them. He struts and sits tall and proud like a king. Rexster made our summer a Rooster Summer. Grandpa gave us a barn kitten to take home, so we can always remember our summer. We call our new cat Summer.

Grandma taught us this funny poem about Rexster:

We have a little rooster, the handsomest ever
    seen.
He washes the dishes and sweeps the house
    clean.
He goes to the mill to fetch us flour
and brings it home in less than an hour.
He bakes us bread and fetches a pail.
He sits by the fire and fans his fine tail.

The End

Now

All this happened some time ago. The farm is gone now. The creek is still there and the railroad tracks run through the land, but the house, barn, chicken coop, Rexster's mulberry tree, even the fields are gone. There are big warehouse buildings, parking lots, a few new trees and concrete where they all used to be.

Now when my sister and I go past the farm and think of the happy "Rooster Summer" we shared, we both feel the sadness that time and change can bring. But we also think of one of Grandma and Grandpa's often-said sayings and how true it is for us:

> *People, places come and go.*
> *But stories, planted, sprout and grow.*